Something Borrowed

YOLANDE KLEINN

Published by
Yolande Kleinn, 2024

www.yolandekleinn.com

Something Borrowed
By Yolande Kleinn

Cover Design: Yolande Kleinn
Cover Photo: Jianxiang Wu
Cover Font: South Signature from thehungryjpeg.com
Cover Font: Antraste from thehungryjpeg.com
Interior Font: Born from thehungryjpeg.com

First Edition January 2024

Print ISBN 978-1-946316-48-6
Digital ISBN 978-1-946316-31-8

– For Mom and Dad –
Thank you for always having my back, even (especially) when life gets complicated.

Chapter One

As the voice droned steadily in his ear, the only thought in Trevor Ortega's head was, *Too bad a stunning location can't salvage an interminable evening.*

He scanned the rooftop garden, taking in the way starlight and a crescent moon glowed across cement pathways and eerily symmetrical greenery. A high stone wall ran the perimeter of the roof, and past it stretched a downtown cityscape reaching all the way to the river and beyond.

Whoever had coaxed their way into using this rooftop bower as a charity venue had seriously outdone themselves.

Understated strings of lights illuminated chairs, white-draped tables, and a long banquet spread, plus a narrow counter where waitstaff served drinks.

The glass of champagne in Trevor's hand was untouched and likely to stay that way. These events wound him too tight to drink. He'd never understood how his fellow attorneys didn't share his reluctance. Tonight's entire tableau felt so starched and formal, so full of people he desperately wanted to impress. After five years settled in as a public defender, he still couldn't imagine relaxing at a gala like this.

The air had cooled considerably now that the sun had set, and even with the extra weight of his nicest suit jacket, Trevor shivered a little. If he could simply appreciate the atmosphere in silence, he might be able to trick himself into enjoying the party.

Of course, silence was more than he could reasonably hope for tonight.

He smiled blandly at the man still talking to him. Trevor had only fleetingly caught the name offered in greeting. He probably should have tried harder to retain the information, if only to avoid crossing paths in the future. Sharp skinny angles gave his relentless conversational partner an intimidating air, the impression not at all helped by aggressive eyebrows and a sweep of receding white hair. The man's expressionless mouth had not stopped moving for ten solid minutes. Trevor hadn't been able to sneak in a single word to excuse himself. Somehow, the other cornered parties had all managed to escape, leaving him the sole recipient of a furious diatribe about the tax code.

Trevor didn't mind conversations about tax codes, as a general rule. They could be fascinating in the right company. But here in this moment, words flowing over him without clarity or inflection, the topic bored him to tears. He couldn't decide if having already eaten made the situation worse or better. On the one hand, he'd be cranky as hell if he were putting up with all this on an empty stomach, waiting in vain for a chance to escape to the banquet line. On the other hand, his full stomach meant the steady lull of his colleague's voice was making him legitimately sleepy.

Ridiculous.

Trevor didn't want to be here in the first place. Now that he'd fulfilled his obligation to make an appearance and could discreetly depart in good conscience, he had no graceful way to extricate himself from a one-sided conversation so dull he would prefer a concussion. It would be a different matter if this were a total stranger—Trevor might be willing to risk interrupting him midword—but he vaguely knew the man as a spouse of someone-or-other whom he couldn't risk offending.

A shadow fell past Trevor's elbow as someone approached him from behind. Even without knowing who the shadow belonged to, an instantaneous rush of relief cut beneath his skin. Any interruption at all could be enough of an opening to enable escape if he played his hand right.

Then he turned—had to tilt his head back to meet the new arrival's eyes—and grinned in recognition.

Sebastian Greer stood at his elbow, tall and broad and unreasonably handsome.

"Trevor." Sebastian greeted him with a nod, then turned an apologetic smile toward the argumentative tax attorney, who had finally stumbled mid-sentence. "Mr. Callum, I hope you'll forgive the intrusion. I've got a professional question for Mr. Ortega. Can I borrow him a moment?"

With difficulty, Trevor contained his grin. If he let it spread too wide, it would broadcast his relief plainly, never mind that he was so grateful for the intervention he could kiss Sebastian here and now.

Thoughts of kissing Sebastian Greer could only lead to incurable distraction and embarrassment if he were caught staring, so Trevor set the notion aside with the efficiency of long practice. He raised his glass in a parting gesture toward Mr. Callum, trying not to appear overly pleased, then let his former boss lead him away.

With every step toward relative seclusion, Trevor tried not to notice how effortlessly gorgeous Sebastian looked in his tuxedo. Wide shoulders filled the dark jacket without straining the fabric. A bow tie sat perfectly knotted under the round line of his jaw, and the crisp white of his collar stood out dramatically against warm umber skin. Sebastian's eyes glittered in the moonlight, and Trevor clenched his teeth.

It wasn't fucking fair. An overworked federal circuit judge had no business looking like he just strode out of a fashion shoot. Even the silvering hair at his temples could have been a touch-up for the cover of a magazine.

How was Trevor supposed to keep his composure in front of a knight in shining armor this devastatingly handsome?

Somehow, whether through willpower or desperation, he managed to tamp down the cascade of uninvited feelings as he and Sebastian reached an empty corner of the roof. Trevor hoped his smile was visible through the shadows and that it conveyed a reasonable level of gratitude.

"Thanks for the rescue."

"Thanks aren't necessary." Sebastian wore a distinctly smug expression as he sipped from the drink in his own hand. It could have been a gin and tonic, but it was probably just club soda with lime. Trevor wasn't the only one who wouldn't risk being inebriated among a crowd of his peers. "I thought I recognized the flicker of glazed displeasure in your eyes. If I misgauged, I offer my sincere apologies."

Trevor snorted at the familiar veneer of decorum in Sebastian's teasing, then sipped his drink to keep from admitting he would forgive nearly anything for the sake of Sebastian's company.

When he trusted himself to manage something more measured than longing, he said, "*Glazed displeasure* might be an understatement. I'd legitimately started to wonder if I should fake a fainting spell to make him go away. I was already scouting for an escape hatch when he cornered me."

Trevor nearly choked on another half-hearted sip of champagne when Sebastian asked, "Can I join your escape attempt? There's an excellent bar half a block away."

Maybe it was silly to be surprised by the suggestion. Sebastian had invited him out for drinks and meals any number of times since their professional paths had parted ways—and in any case, the invitation was never for anything more intimate than a casual evening between colleagues, no matter how fervently Trevor might wish otherwise. They'd never socialized off the clock while he was Sebastian's law clerk, but the five years since had been different. Trevor didn't think he'd imagined the way they had slipped gradually across the line from professional acquaintances to friends.

"God, yes, *please* let's do that." He prayed his helpless infatuation didn't echo too obviously through the words.

*

The place was a perfect low-key balm after the stiff formality of the fundraiser. It was noisy enough to let Trevor and Sebastian blend into their surroundings but not so packed they couldn't find a table. The decor was a little snooty for Trevor's tastes—mirrors all over the place and lights in intricate sconces along the walls—but the boisterous crowd more than made up for a stodgy first impression.

There were a couple of empty stools at the bar, but Trevor homed right in on a table in a far corner. Never mind that it was so small he and Sebastian would be stepping on each other's toes, it was also at exactly the right remove from surrounding conversations and laughter, close to but not swallowed by the room's rowdy energy.

Sebastian followed without protest, and both of them slid into metal chairs with ornate patterns shaped into the backs. A laminated drink menu proclaimed all kinds of local brews available.

"Loon Juice for me," Trevor said when a server came to take their orders, both because he wanted to say it out loud and because cider sounded fantastic after his untouched dry champagne from the fundraiser.

"Do you have Summit Summer Ale on tap?" At the answering nod, Sebastian said, "A pint of that, please."

Then it was blessedly just the two of them, isolated in their little pocket of a lively downtown bar. Trevor tried to be discreet about watching Sebastian in the low, warm light. The crisp edges of fancy dress seemed to have softened with the change to a more casual locale. The bow tie had vanished during the short span of their journey, the black jacket fallen open. The topmost buttons of Sebastian's collar were undone in deference to the room's cozy heat.

Trevor might have been imagining the way Sebastian watched him back for a moment—impossible to confirm when he was busy averting his own gaze. He wondered what Sebastian saw looking at him. Skinny shoulders, sharp nose, big eyes that had never successfully bluffed through a single poker hand. Dark hair in need of a cut, styled to within an inch of its life because he hadn't been willing to take any chances with the wind. His suit was a little outdated, but he knew it fit him handsomely.

The fact that Trevor had put excessive care into his appearance didn't mean Sebastian was the sort of man to appreciate the presentation. Trevor had no idea if Sebastian was interested in men, despite years of agonizing over the question. He'd never met anyone more circumspect about their personal life than Sebastian Goddamn Greer.

Their drinks arrived quickly. And then another round, along with a basket of perfectly seasoned tater tots. It didn't take long for Trevor to be glad he'd taken a taxi to the gala and wouldn't be driving. Hell, maybe he and Sebastian could share a cab home.

Or maybe that was a thought Trevor needed to avoid at all costs.

He'd honed a talent for multitasking his entire life, and still this hiccup of distraction threatened to derail his focus on the current conversation. Losing an argument to Sebastian wouldn't be especially embarrassing, nor would it be novel. But Trevor was *right* this time, damn it, and he rerouted his attention back to the debate where it belonged.

"You're missing the point. Deliberately." Trevor delivered his retort with an expansive gesture.

The glint in Sebastian's eyes suggested he was simply playing devil's advocate—that he knew exactly the point Trevor was *trying* to make—and something that might have been a smirk twitched at one corner of his mouth.

Trevor tried to ignore all of this and stay on track. "It's not about whether the prosecutor can find a fucking hearsay exception applicable to the situation. It's not hearsay in the first place, it—"

He stopped abruptly when another emphatic hand gesture nearly upset his drink—a full glass, probably his last of the evening. The corner of Sebastian's mouth twitched higher, and God, the expression made Trevor's insides heat. The number of times Sebastian had looked at him the same way, back when they worked together, took up far too much space in Trevor's memory. Never mocking, more conspiratorial, the expression mingled amusement with an unmistakable invitation to share in the laugh. As a law clerk with no business falling for his handsome and staggeringly competent judge, Trevor had found himself repeatedly floored.

He'd spent a lot of time in chambers telling himself to calm the fuck down.

It worked just as well now as it had then. He resisted the instinct to launch directly back into his abandoned rant. It was a near mathematical certainty that Sebastian already agreed with him and was pushing Trevor's buttons on purpose, never mind that Trevor couldn't fathom why. The man always had seemed to enjoy goading him into spirited debate, all the while rebutting each point with far too much skill, a couple incisive words enough to muddle Trevor's entire argument.

Then again, there was a reason Sebastian was considered one of the best judges in the district. And there was a reason Trevor had wanted to work solely for Sebastian Greer, back when he'd been finishing law school and should have been casting the widest possible net for job opportunities. The industry was stacked against him in a lot of ways, many of them technically illegal and slow to change. Plenty of doors actively *tried* not to open for a man with his name and unmistakably brown skin. The smart thing would've been to apply for as many jobs as possible and not risk ending up underemployed with a mountain of debt to pay off.

But something had told him the county courthouse was exactly where he belonged, and even before he'd met the man—even before he'd had the chance to fall head over heels like a fool—Trevor had been certain he needed to work with Sebastian Greer.

The bar quieted a little around them, and Trevor tore his gaze from Sebastian's face with difficulty. He fished out his phone as a pretext for breaking eye contact and checked the time. Late, but not so late he felt any need to cut things short and call a cab. He opened his email to stall for time, not yet braced to meet Sebastian's beautiful brown eyes without showing his whole damn soul.

Trevor froze at the new message sitting at the top of his inbox. The subject line stopped him in his tracks.

You Are Cordially Invited to the Wedding of Emma Calcaterra and Sloane Smith...

The words were a perfect mirror to the paper invitation he'd received in the mail over a month ago. The reminder in his inbox felt like a slap on the wrist, though of course Emma would never intend it to be cruel. The digital nudge was probably a practical necessity. Trevor hadn't RSVP'd, mostly because he'd been trying not to think about his ex-girlfriend's pending nuptials. He should have expected her to push a little harder. This wasn't a pity invite. Strange as Trevor might feel about maintaining an amicable relationship after parting ways with his only serious significant other, Emma sincerely wanted him to attend.

He tapped the message and found the email included a link to an online portal. He wouldn't even have to track down the official postcard to RSVP. Would he be attending? Did he plan to bring a plus-one?

For a guilty moment, Trevor wasn't sure he could bear to go.

The painful truth was, he didn't want to. The thought of being present to witness the former love of his life marrying his law school rival… It sucked. He'd rather be happy for them at a safe remove. He missed Emma. He wanted her to be happy. He harbored no delusions about any old twinges of romantic feeling; Trevor found it difficult to obsess over an ex while falling inextricably in love with someone else.

But attending her wedding single and alone did not sound like a good time.

A sinking sensation settled into his stomach as he realized none of this reasoning mattered. Of course he would attend.

"What's wrong?" Sebastian's quiet question cut through the spiral of emotional upheaval, and Trevor sat straighter with a start.

His first, almost overpowering instinct was to brush off the offered concern. He felt ridiculous for being upset over something relatively trivial. After five years establishing his own separate career, he still hated the idea of Sebastian thinking him ridiculous.

But damn it, Sebastian wasn't just a former employer. He was a *friend.* There were few people in the world Trevor truly trusted, and Sebastian had long since earned his place in the lineup.

"My ex-girlfriend is getting married, and I'm short a plus-one to the wedding."

One of Sebastian's eyebrows rose in obvious confusion. "You're invited to your ex's wedding? And you intend to go?"

"Of course I'm going."

Sebastian paused significantly before observing, "You don't seem happy about it."

Too much careful sympathy echoed beneath the words. Sincerity, worry, maybe even a faint sheen of protectiveness. Trevor's every defensive instinct kicked into high gear at the thought of this man—friend, mentor, former boss, center of every romantic fantasy he'd harbored for years—pitying him. He needed to rearrange the landscape before things turned too serious to salvage.

He couldn't brush the entire conversation aside. Sebastian knew him too well for blunt obfuscation to do the trick. But surely he could steer the discussion into less gloomy territory.

"What I need," Trevor said with what he hoped was convincing cheer, "is a stand-in date. A fake partner to make me look good for the night."

This time, Sebastian's answer came with unaccustomed caution. "I'm sure you're acquainted with any number of women who'd be willing to assist you."

Trevor blinked, startled at an observation that felt not only heteronormative but *deliberately* so. "It doesn't have to be a woman." He shrugged, the gesture calculated to convey a lightness the statement didn't actually contain.

"Emma knows I'm no straighter than she is. I could borrow a boyfriend for the wedding just as easy, assuming I had any damn volunteers."

For an instant Sebastian's eyes widened—a flash that made it clear he'd somehow missed this personal detail during their years of acquaintance—but he seemed more at ease when he said, "More potential candidates, then." He raised his glass in a half-hearted toast. "Surely finding someone won't be too daunting."

"Yeah." A hint of Trevor's previous morose tone snuck into the word, despite his best efforts to stay upbeat.

"Not to ask the nosy question," Sebastian spoke in the same uncharacteristically hesitant tone, "but why can't you go alone?"

"I could." Trevor slouched in his seat, abandoning the cheerful facade. "It shouldn't matter. I just... It was my fault things fell apart with Emma. I was a wreck during law school. It's great she found someone amazing, but the thought of showing up to this thing alone..."

The fact that Emma was marrying *Sloane*—the smart, ambitious, infuriatingly perfect woman who had edged him out for managing editor of the law review journal—wasn't the problem. The problem was all him. He would probably spend the rest of his life feeling guilty about letting Emma down. It had nothing to do with wanting her back. He'd let go of any such urge a long time ago, but the guilt clung to him, stubborn and strong.

No relationship ever survived law school completely unscathed, but Trevor had failed harder than most at balancing his priorities. The lesson had ultimately penetrated, but not in time to salvage his deteriorating relationship.

He couldn't bear to spell these details out for Sebastian, no matter how complete his reservoir of trust. He hated what a frantic mess he'd become by his third and final year of school. The friendships damaged during those awful months were still recovering, and he didn't blame anyone for cutting ties.

He couldn't condemn Emma for walking away.

Sebastian sat perfectly motionless, either waiting for further explanation or giving Trevor time to collect himself.

Trevor drew a slow breath. "Emma's family was judgmental as hell even when we were together. Condescending rich assholes, y'know? It's stupid, but I don't want their pity." Or their scorn, for that matter. Trevor couldn't be sure which was more likely, but he didn't want to find out.

Silence held for a very long time—long enough that Trevor had to fight the urge to fidget beneath the weight of Sebastian's considering stare—before any answer came.

"I think I understand."

"Yeah." Trevor figured Sebastian would get it. The man had always been a good listener.

"Do you...know who you'll ask?" Sebastian's question came with a faint hitch of awkwardness, but Trevor didn't take it personally. This topic swept way outside their usual conversational bounds. For all the ease of their interactions since parting ways professionally, they'd never discussed romance. They'd never come close. Sebastian had always been too private and close-lipped on the subject.

And Trevor had been terrified his crush would show through.

He shook his head and then propped his chin on one hand. "Emma and I have too many overlapping social circles." His best friend might be game under different circumstances, but Emma and Cam went all the way back to high school. There were too many points of intersection, and the cleanup would be a disaster. "It needs to be someone Emma doesn't know, or there's no point."

"You must have some friends who fit the bill."

Trevor huffed a frustrated sigh. "You're my friend. Will you go with me?" The words came out of nowhere, uninvited and unforgivably brash. The second they were out of his mouth, Trevor wanted to take them back. *Fuck.* What lovesick nonsense was this? How could he have thought the question, let alone spoken it aloud? He already felt pathetic, admitting so many vulnerable truths. What would Sebastian think now?

Sebastian's eyes widened, but the flicker of shock faded quickly. Another moment and the expression resolved into something considering.

Trevor held his breath, too stunned to withdraw the question. He didn't dare hope. This couldn't possibly go where his suddenly racing heart wanted to imagine.

"Okay," Sebastian said. Simple. Blunt. He sounded surprised—as though he couldn't quite believe he was agreeing—but the word held no hint of reluctance.

A zing of electricity crackled along Trevor's spine, and he straightened in his seat. "Really?"

"I've never met Emma, or any other Calcaterra. I'm up for a bit of subterfuge."

"That's—" Trevor had to stop. Swallow. Breathe. "Yeah. Okay. Great. You— We can— I'll forward you the information."

Later. Maybe tomorrow. After his head and heart and entire world stopped spinning.

Chapter Two

Trevor woke the next morning with a rotten taste in his mouth and a dull headache. The low throbbing was less a proper hangover than a reminder that he should have chugged an extra glass of water last night. Sitting up eased the worst of the tension at his temples, and swallowing a couple of painkillers helped gradually with the rest.

Distracted as he was by the sullen state of his head, it took the better part of an hour for memory of last night's conversation to present itself.

Trevor froze when the recollection hit him, immediate and bright. Not just posing the question, but *forwarding the invitation*, apparently too impatient to wait on a few hours' sleep and a sober head. He'd been tipsy and warm, riding the adrenaline rush of Sebastian's *yes*—and it'd taken only a moment to send his digital RSVP.

It didn't feel real. He fumbled for his phone, suddenly desperate to figure out if he'd actually forwarded the details to Sebastian.

No need to dig down into the sent-messages folder to find his answer. There, right at the top of a crowded inbox, sat a reply with Sebastian Greer's name on it. Trevor clicked through and read with mounting disbelief. The message confirmed in the stiffly formal tone of all Sebastian's emails that he was free the relevant evening. That he would drive over to pick Trevor up, unless some other mode of travel would be better. And that he'd plan on wearing a plain black suit unless Trevor preferred to coordinate.

A dozen straightforward practicalities, yet the email left Trevor breathless. The entire situation felt more like a fever dream than something that was actually happening to him. Half an hour later, as he fried a couple eggs and brewed a pot of coffee, several complications occurred to him simultaneously.

First and most important: Emma never having met Sebastian didn't guarantee she wouldn't recognize his name. Sebastian had made himself a prominent figure in the legal community, and Emma knew a whole lot of lawyers. Hell, she was marrying one. Her family compounded the problem: an alarming proportion of them were attorneys practicing right in the metro area.

Second: Emma's contingent wouldn't be the only crowd at this wedding. Trevor didn't know Sloane Smith in any close personal way, but her family might possess inconvenient connections. Not to mention all the mutual acquaintances he would surely run into.

None of those acquaintances had ever met Sebastian—Trevor was reasonably confident on this point—but many would recognize the name. And, of course, there was Trevor's nosy best friend, who knew all about the battered state of his obstinate heart, even if Trevor had never actually said the words aloud. If Trevor somehow managed to reach the day of the wedding without fessing up, Cameron Vance would take one look at this debacle and throw his hands up in exasperation.

If Trevor actually went through with this, introductions would earn him plenty of raised eyebrows. Worse, he would have to follow his party trick with a fictitious breakup. The only alternative was to tell the retroactive truth to a handful of people and let the gossip spread. Neither strategy held any particular appeal, and both were rife with inevitable awkwardness.

The only reasonable choice was to tell Sebastian he'd changed his mind and would attend the wedding solo after all.

But reasonable or not, Trevor couldn't do it. Something had taken root in his chest since last night. Forget Emma's family and their close-minded snobbery. No threat of awkwardness could overcome the selfish appeal of attending this wedding with Sebastian beside him. Close proximity and dancing, the deliberate illusion that he and Sebastian were more than simple colleagues.

This would be either heaven or torture. Trevor couldn't decide which, but he was suddenly desperate to find out.

*

He remained in a tumult through the next several days, focusing on his heavy caseload and looming deadlines. Dinner with Cameron snuck up on him. They'd made the plans a week ago, but most nonwork details had fled Trevor's mind in the wake of his pact with Sebastian Greer.

Thank God Cam was the type to send check-in texts. When the message pinged Trevor's phone—*still on tonight?*—all he had to do was send an affirmative response to hide the fact that he'd completely forgotten.

As usual, Cam beat him to their favorite overcrowded bar and grill. Cam always arrived first, no matter where they went or what they did. Instead of asking to put his name on the list for a table, Trevor ducked farther into the restaurant in search of his friend.

He found Cam at a booth in the far corner, already working through a basket of fries with a barely-touched pint in front of him. Trevor slid onto the empty bench across the table and loosened his tie as he reached for the drink menu. He hadn't yet decided whether he would unburden himself of recent anxieties or try to pretend nothing was amiss. Maybe he could hide behind the long list of local brews and keep avoiding Cam's eyes forever.

Impossible, of course. Trevor wasn't surprised when Cam only waited two seconds before pitching a question over the din of the bar.

"What did you do?"

Trevor raised his head and found Cam watching him with narrowed eyes.

"Huh?" It wasn't an especially eloquent evasion, and of course it didn't work.

"You're wearing that look. The one you're gonna swear up, down, and sideways isn't guilt even though you can barely look at me. Which means you fucked up and don't want to admit it." Cam delivered this analysis with irrefutable confidence.

Only now, after being blatantly called out, did Trevor realize how desperately he had hoped to fly under the radar with his conundrum. It was a foolish hope no matter how he framed it. After all, Cam would be at the wedding.

A server approached, granting Trevor a short reprieve to order a glass of merlot and a cheeseburger. Then the server vanished, and he found himself alone once more with the piercing, infuriatingly patient weight of his best friend's stare. Cam hadn't stopped watching him. There was no escaping the searchlight of such intense attention.

"*Talk*," Cam commanded when Trevor's silence persisted.

There was no point demurring. Cam knew him better than anyone. Hell, Cameron Vance was the sole friendship Trevor hadn't managed to bulldoze during law school—largely because Cam's grad school studies abroad had been equally overwhelming. With both of them walking disasters focused on school to the detriment of all else, it had been remarkably easy to reconnect in the spaces between. Those spaces may have been few, but they allowed enough breathing room for true friendship to rekindle once they'd gotten their shit together.

Of course Cam could smell the distraction on Trevor from a mile away. It was a foregone conclusion that Trevor would confess every embarrassing detail of his lapse in judgment.

There was no minimizing the outrageous fact of what he'd done, so he dove in with total candor. "I invited Sebastian Greer to Emma's wedding and asked him to pretend we're a couple for the night." Fuck. It sounded worse out loud than it did in his head. He wanted to hide behind a menu again, but the server had taken them all away.

"Ah," Cam said, as though this explanation made perfect sense. "And he said no. So now you're freaking out about asking him in the first place."

"He said yes." The words escaped Trevor's mouth so fast he couldn't have reined them in if he wanted to. At least his dubious pride had the consolation of watching Cam's eyes flash comically wide.

"He— Wait. What?"

"Sebastian agreed to attend Emma's wedding as my plus-one to back me up."

"And to impersonate your fraudulent boyfriend," Cam deadpanned.

Trevor managed not to flinch. "I prefer to think of the situation as 'borrowing' rather than 'fraud.'"

"It doesn't matter what you *call it*. He's not your boyfriend!" Cam unsettled his pint glass with this exasperated outburst, though it was heavy enough not to tip over. "Which. Fuck. I have so many questions. Starting with, how did you convince him to go along with this? And ending with, *why*?"

"I can't go to Emma and Sloane's wedding without a date." Trevor prayed he wouldn't need to argue this point. Cam, of all people, knew how much baggage underpinned the situation. He'd been in Scotland during the most dramatic moments of Trevor's time in law school, but he also knew every detail about the breakup—the only friend Trevor had convinced himself to confide in.

Equally important, Cam knew all about Sloane Smith, the one member of Trevor's law school cohort poised to kick his ass at every turn. The very first week of classes, she'd eviscerated him in a spontaneous oral argument. Their Con Law professor had let the discussion play out uninterrupted—until Trevor's reasoning had been reduced to a cratered mess—and then the class had moved along as though the entire exercise wasn't worth acknowledging.

Trevor couldn't remember what the argument had been about, but it didn't matter. The humiliation was memorable enough.

Their first collision had set the tone for the next three years. Sloane was never cruel. She was just alarmingly, overwhelmingly smart. Impossibly thorough. Trevor made a point of never allowing himself to be trounced so handily again, but every subsequent interaction was a contest of equal intensity. When she'd narrowly beaten him out for top editor of the school's law review journal, Trevor's pricked pride had nearly flattened him.

He occasionally wished she were an awful person. Then he could at least figure out how to hate her. But Sloane Smith was fundamentally kind, and there was nothing Trevor could do about that.

Just like there was nothing he could do to stop her from marrying his ex-girlfriend. With all his heart, he wanted good things for Emma Calcaterra, but damn it. In all the wide world of people Emma could have fallen for, why did it have to be Sloane?

Deep as he'd settled into these sullen memories, Trevor jolted when Cam's voice dragged him back to the present.

"Fine. Let's postulate that you can't admit you're single at Emma's wedding." Cam spoke with the dry tones of a man who clearly considered the opposite to be true, suggesting Trevor *could* attend alone and these theatrics were unnecessary. "*This* you consider a reasonable alternative? *Pretending to date your former boss*?"

"It seemed like a good idea when I asked him." Trevor glared at the table so hard he startled when a glass of red wine appeared in his field of vision, set down so smoothly the server was already gone by the time he raised his head. He took the glass in hand and let a first slow sip linger on his tongue. The wine was mediocre at best, but he savored it anyway, biding his time.

A pointed silence stretched across the table toward Trevor. When he set his glass down, the silence lingered within their dubious bubble of privacy. Disbelief undercut the silence. Restaurant patrons and servers passed by, loud conversations brushing past at close range but never quite breaching the illusion of solitude.

Trevor suspected Cam was waiting for further justifications, but he didn't speak. Even if he'd wanted to defend himself, he wouldn't know where to start.

"Are you still in love with him?" Cam asked in a voice so low it barely carried over the din.

Trevor straightened stiffly in his seat, staring into Cam's eyes, frozen and appalled at hearing the words. Trevor had never spoken anything near those sentiments aloud. They were too much, and he was halfway offended to hear them come so easily out of Cam's mouth. Yes, his infatuation had crossed a threshold years ago, and yes, his best friend had long since sussed out the truth. But that was no reason for Cam to call him out like this, over something Trevor had never technically admitted.

"Who says I'm in love with him?"

Cam's answering expression was both pitying and exasperated. It also reflected a maddening gleam of protective affection.

Cam held his tongue with obvious difficulty as the server returned with two plates of food, massive burgers garnished with even more fries. Only once they were alone again did Cam continue.

"We've known each other forever, and I've *seen you* in love. I was there when you started dating Emma, and I saw what a wreck you were after the breakup. You think I don't recognize what this is?"

Trevor didn't want to think about his breakup with Emma, so far in the past it felt like a separate lifetime. He'd come a long way in the years since then, sorted out his priorities, learned how to balance professional ambition with friendships and a personal life. All of this had been hard won, but he'd gotten there.

Abruptly, Trevor realized it wasn't merely pride driving this decision. His complicated relationship with Sloane Smith and the acidic notion of Emma's parents discomfited him, but they weren't the main problem.

He needed *Emma* to see that he was okay. The most vivid memory he carried from their breakup was a glint of something too close to pity in her eyes.

Cam shook his head as though reading these exact thoughts written across Trevor's face. "You don't have anything to prove. Not to Emma, and not to anyone else."

"It's not about proving myself." Trevor tried to find the right words to make Cam back off without sacrificing his few remaining defenses. "It's about making sure she doesn't worry about me, because she will. Even when she was *breaking up with me*, she was worried." It had galled him at the time. He'd been defensive and angry, a tumult of feelings wrapped up in ugly heartbreak.

The knowledge ached differently now, but he couldn't let her pity him again.

"That sounds like her problem to deal with," Cam said.

Trevor swallowed hard, trying to dislodge the lump in his throat. "Can we talk about something else?"

"No." Cam's brows lowered ominously. "You have answered zero of my questions."

"I told you why I'm doing this."

"You—" Cam huffed a frustrated exhale. "Okay. Fine. That's one answer. But why the fuck is Sebastian going along with it?"

"Because he's a good friend?" Trevor tried to keep his tone breezy.

"*I'm* a good friend. And I'm telling you this convoluted plan is a bad idea."

Trevor had no real rebuttal despite his talent for arguing. Cam's analysis was sound. Even worse, thinking about it too closely made Trevor's world spin and his head hurt, so he pushed the whole tangle aside.

"It's one night. I can fess up later, and Emma will be too amused to get angry."

"Probably true," Cam conceded with obvious reluctance. The furrow at the center of his brow exaggerated the downward turn of his mouth. "But I'm not worried about Emma. She isn't the one who's spent the better part of a decade obsessed with Sebastian Greer. Why are you torturing yourself?"

Trevor bit his tongue to keep from answering truthfully. *Because this is the closest I'll ever get. Because I'm not strong enough to turn down something I've wanted so badly and for so long, even if it's a farce. Because sometimes my heart overrides my better judgment.*

Because Sebastian agreed to go, and how the fuck am I supposed to walk away from that?

It would only be a few hours. And yes, maybe he had set himself up for a whirlwind of Cinderella bullshit, but he could pull this off. Surely he was capable of keeping it together for one night and then starting over the next day with his heart intact, or at least rebuilding whatever was left.

"I know what I'm doing," he said and prayed it wasn't a lie.

Chapter Three

"Are you all right?" Sebastian asked as Trevor settled into the passenger seat and buckled in. "You look jittery."

Trevor smoothed his suit jacket—a rented tuxedo—under the seatbelt to avoid creases, then gave what he hoped resembled a careless shrug. "I'm a little nervous about seeing Emma." It wasn't exactly a lie. It just wasn't the entire truth.

The arrival of Emma's wedding day had Trevor sincerely off-balance. Sebastian didn't need to know about his own part in causing Trevor's restless energy, a whirlwind roiling somewhere between eagerness and apprehension.

Sebastian made a sympathetic noise, then fell quiet long enough to navigate away from Trevor's apartment. It wasn't until they'd traveled halfway to the wedding venue that he said, "We should probably discuss strategy before we arrive. Or at least consider the limits of our ruse." He didn't look at Trevor as he spoke, focused instead on the just-past-rush-hour traffic around them. But his tone was relaxed, the words casual.

Trevor glanced over, trying to read beneath the serene surface. He'd long since memorized the lines of Sebastian's handsome face. The thick eyebrows and broad nose, the high cheekbones, the ever-present quirk of a smile. Subtle mischief glinted in Sebastian's eyes tonight, visible even in profile.

It seemed ridiculous, in retrospect, that Trevor had ever mistaken his fascination with Sebastian for professional admiration. At the very beginning of his clerkship, when he was still insisting to himself that the warm attachment in his chest was simple hero worship—that it would fade with familiarity and routine—he should have recognized the lie. Now, taking in the crinkle at the corner of Sebastian's eye, affection surged so brightly it took him a moment to remember he should say something.

Maybe this was a terrible idea after all. How could he hope to keep it together through the reception if he couldn't manage the trick in the privacy of Sebastian's car? They weren't even pretending to be a couple yet. Trevor couldn't possibly maintain the illusion that all of this was completely normal, in public and through a lengthy evening.

"Are you really okay with all this?" Trevor blurted.

Sebastian's relaxed expression instantly stiffened. "Of course I am. I wouldn't have volunteered otherwise. Why?" A flicker of a glance was all Sebastian could spare from the passing traffic, but it was enough to convey a wary new edge of hesitation. "Have you changed your mind?"

If Trevor didn't know better, he might have mistaken the tone of the question for disappointment. He tucked the irrational ember of hope down deep, squashing it into a corner where it couldn't wound him.

"No." He wasn't strong enough to make a course correction now. "I'm game. Just feeling guilty for dragging you into this mess."

A hint of the tension in Sebastian's shoulders eased. "Don't worry about me. I'm looking forward to the challenge."

A quick bark of laughter escaped Trevor's throat. Sebastian sounded downright smug, and the tone sent a giddy new sensation along Trevor's nerves. For a fleeting instant, Sebastian glanced over, the crow's feet at the corners of his eyes creasing more noticeably than before. The glance didn't last a full second before turning back to the road, but it was plenty of time for Trevor's face to heat and pulse to race.

Forget the rest of the evening. How was he going to survive the rest of the drive?

"So?" Sebastian didn't seem to notice Trevor's winded silence. "What's our strategy? A romantic relationship implies certain behaviors. We'll need at least a modicum of physical contact to sell the fiction. I'd prefer to go in knowing what you're comfortable with."

"Right." Trevor's face flushed hotter than ever. "That's… Yeah. I mean, pretty much anything is okay. We're going to be in public; there's only so much we can… Nothing you do is likely to freak me out." God, he needed to stop talking. His usual eloquence had deserted him, and in its absence, he was right on the verge of humiliating himself.

"I'd just as soon define specific boundaries." Sebastian chuckled wryly, tone carrying a faint suggestion of strain. "The fewer surprises the better. I'm pretty sure that's rule number one for going undercover."

"We're not going undercover. We're pretending to be boyfriends."

Sebastian shrugged. "The point stands."

Trevor considered the question, glad Sebastian wasn't watching as his blush blazed to new extremes. "You can cuddle up pretty close. I'm not shy."

"Hold hands? Kiss on the cheek?"

Amazingly, Trevor managed normal speech. "Sure. Those things are fine." Thinking about Sebastian's mouth anywhere near him sent helpless shivers along his skin. His hands trembled a little as he resisted the urge to clench them into fists. Fucking hell, he had to get his heart rate down. Anyone would think he was a teenager suffering his first unrequited crush.

That wasn't a fair comparison, though. Trevor's first teenage crush hadn't left him nearly this flustered.

"Obviously, you're welcome to do the same," Sebastian added, thorough as always.

"Thanks." Trevor swallowed hard, trying not to think about what a wrecked puddle he would be by the end of the night. "That's— Absolutely. I will. Whatever sells the story." As to the bludgeoning his poor, shameless heart would take in the process...

Trevor would just have to glue the pieces back together tomorrow.

*

The ceremony was fine.

Except "fine" wasn't the right word at all. Emma's wedding was elaborate, and long, and expensive as hell. Sloane, in her crisp white dress, and Emma, in her sleek tuxedo, could have stepped directly out of a fairy tale. Trevor sat patiently through a full mass, surrounded by more guests than he could begin to count, the entire thing a carefully coordinated spectacle.

He recognized Emma's taste in so many delicate details, despite all the pageantry, and thought maybe he could spot some of Sloane's too. Neither woman was the sort to get railroaded by other people's expectations. It was an impressive feat, the way they'd crafted something so personal and heartfelt out of what could easily have been a complete circus of extravagance.

The receiving line put him in a twitchy mood—right up to the moment Sebastian took his hand and simply held it. The gesture grounded him more solidly than it had any right to, and Trevor was breathing easier by the time they drew close enough to congratulate Emma and Sloane.

Both brides examined Trevor's date with blatant curiosity as he introduced them, Emma grinning and Sloane watchful in her alarmingly canny way. Trevor prayed she wasn't seeing straight through the ruse. There wasn't a damn thing he could do about the possibility, so he quashed a fresh jangle of nerves and leaned his weight against Sebastian as subtly as he could. The tightness in his chest eased when Sebastian responded by letting go of his hand to drape a protective arm across his shoulders.

Trevor exhaled as he tucked in close along Sebastian's side. Together they moved forward, making way for the people behind them in line.

Flowery signage guided them toward an adjacent property for the reception, directly behind the church. Trevor tried to be stealthy about snugging in tighter along Sebastian's side as they stepped through a set of ornate double doors and down onto a narrow sidewalk.

The sun had set during the lengthy wedding mass, which left the outdoor reception venue swathed in soft darkness. Perfectly rectangular hedges lined the yard on one side. On the other, a chaotic collection of trees and shrubs marked the edge of a separate garden. Strings of warm light threaded all around the yard, illuminating rows of tables and a vast dance floor, but they were almost unnecessary. The night sky shone perfectly clear, and starlight mingled mischievously with a luminous full moon.

Grudgingly, Trevor had to concede this was a beautiful place to celebrate.

"Oh dear," Sebastian murmured, arm slipping down from Trevor's shoulders. A disappointing chill followed the unexpected absence. A moment later, Sebastian's hand settled at the small of his back. An equally reassuring touch but decidedly more discreet, and Trevor belatedly realized why the sudden shift.

He recognized the man approaching them across the lawn, tall and broad, with a round face and rounder stomach, strikingly handsome in a perfectly tailored suit. Dark brown skin contrasted with a pale-blue necktie. His face, so similar to Sebastian's, offered a smile that rendered his features even more charming.

"Josiah Greer!" Trevor extended his hand, hopefully quick enough to disguise the outburst as a greeting. "Hi."

"Mr. Ortega." Sebastian's brother had a powerful, though not deliberately intimidating, grip. It felt more like he was modulating an excess of strength rather than attempting to make an aggressive impression. His smile widened, his dark eyes glittering with questions as he took in how close together Sebastian and Trevor stood. "A pleasure as always. And it's good to see you, Sebastian. I meant to tell you I'll be in town for a couple days."

Trevor had only met Josiah a handful of times, but he carried a positive estimation of the man. He nodded amiably along, not really paying attention to the content of the exchange—he was too busy trying to figure out why Sebastian's brother might be here. If there was some connection to the Calcaterras, Trevor had completely missed it.

He didn't catch Sebastian's question, but it must have mirrored Trevor's thoughts, because Josiah answered, "Sloane was a mentee of mine during her college days. We stayed in touch." Curiosity glittered in the look he gave Sebastian. "I must admit, I didn't expect to run into you here."

"I'm a plus-one." Sebastian's tone remained impressively blithe. "I'm not acquainted with either bride."

"Hmm." Josiah glanced between them as though taking time to absorb this information. "And you two are here together?"

Before either Trevor or Sebastian could answer, someone called for Josiah from the front cluster of circular tables. With an apologetic glance and a small bow, Josiah moved off toward the summons. A temporary reprieve, but Trevor was grateful regardless. He sucked in a hard breath before letting it out in a sheepish laugh.

"That was unexpected," Sebastian agreed.

"Guess I won't be the only one doing damage control after tonight." Trevor tried to keep his tone light. He must have succeeded at least a little, judging by Sebastian's wry chuckle.

Their assigned table, when at last they reached it, was packed with fellow guests who ranged from complete strangers to people Trevor knew in passing. Cameron Vance, sitting next to two empty seats, was the only truly familiar face. He gave Sebastian a confounded once-over but otherwise evinced no surprise on seeing them together. For a quick instant, Cam's gaze dropped to their joined hands before rising again. His eyebrows arched eloquently up to his hairline.

Sebastian let go of Trevor's hand, and then that warm palm pressed to the small of his back again. Grounding pressure. The contact was welcome and steady and deceptively casual.

Trevor smiled and looked his friend directly in the eye, willing him to play along. "Cam, you've met Sebastian, haven't you?" Then, still standing, he coordinated introductions with the unfamiliar rest of the table. He didn't bother spelling out the ruse. Their proximity made it clear Sebastian was here as his date.

As he tried to memorize names to go with the collection of new and vaguely recognized faces, Trevor could feel Cam's stare drilling into the side of his head. Curiosity blinked at him from other eyes, too, since at least some of these guests knew who he and Sebastian were. He had no obligation to answer their unspoken questions or explain how a former law clerk might have started dating his judge.

But Cam was a different matter. Trevor hadn't expected to face more questions from this quarter, but he also couldn't ignore the wordless urgency emanating toward him.

It was cruel to abandon Sebastian to this table full of strangers, but Trevor couldn't express himself candidly here. He gave Cam a long, deliberate look before turning once more to his date.

For a moment, he got distracted by Sebastian's eyes. Ochre-brown, with equal parts query and worry, they caught and held him so intensely it took several heartbeats to remember his plan. By the time Trevor recovered himself, he'd been staring too long. He needed to cover his lapse.

Bracing himself for a maneuver so brazen he couldn't quite believe he was doing it, Trevor rose onto his toes and pressed a quick kiss to Sebastian's cheek. "I'll get us drinks." Then he turned away from the table, ignoring the frantic hammering of his heart.

Cam's chair scooted back. "I'll go with you."

As they departed, Trevor heard someone ask, "So, Sebastian, how on earth did you and Trevor meet?"

He almost turned around to run interference, but Sebastian was already answering. "I don't really like to discuss such things. I'm a terrible storyteller." The tone carried a gentle shutdown, and Trevor snorted as he continued his retreat. Hopefully, the evasion would dissuade anyone else from asking personal questions for which he and Sebastian had done nothing to prepare.

Once Trevor's path carried him far enough from the tables—out into the open at a distance from any potential eavesdroppers—Cam locked him with a piercing stare.

"I honestly didn't think you'd go through with it."

Trevor straightened his spine as a zing of defensiveness coursed through him. "Why wouldn't I?"

"Because it's still a bad idea. I hoped you'd think about everything I said and talk yourself out of this. And instead, here you are, even more of a wreck than I expected."

"I am not a wreck." But as Trevor spoke the words, he knew they weren't true. Agitation coiled inside him, the raw edge of too many feelings wrapping around his heart, ready to crush him when he and Sebastian inevitably went their separate ways.

"Trevor." A cajoling note touched the syllables. Cam sounded genuinely worried, and the realization drew Trevor up short.

He relaxed the hands he hadn't noticed clenching at his sides. "I'm fine."

"You're not." Cam shook his head. "What are you doing, man?"

Sheepish and a little bit lost, Trevor finally admitted, "I don't know."

Chapter Four

He did not bother collecting the promised drinks but returned to his seat just in time for the DJ to call for quiet. The wedding party filed out into the settling twilight, accompanied by music so loud it made Trevor's temples throb.

The thudding bass line only exacerbated the complicated way his heart clenched on seeing the newlyweds emerge hand in hand. They stood perfectly still on the topmost church step, framed by the open doorway. The photographer snapped a photo of them bathed in golden light—Sloane's warm brown skin a perfect contrast to the crisp lines of her dress, her hair braided high on her head—Emma's tuxedo sharp and smart, her pale cheeks flushed with excitement.

Trevor had never seen Emma so happy. She stood there beaming until a new song began, and then she and her wife at last descended the stairs.

"Are you okay?" Sebastian leaned in close to be audible over the music and cheering. It had to be unintentional, the way his lips brushed the shell of Trevor's ear, but the contact made him shiver pleasantly.

"I'm fine." He hated that the words didn't ring entirely truthful.

He was happy for Emma and reasonably confident jealousy was not among his complicated reactions. He didn't wish he were standing there in Sloane's place. But there was a twisting sensation in his chest, a roil in his stomach, and Trevor didn't know what to make of these things.

He started at a warm touch covering his hand as the wedding party began their speeches. Of course it was Sebastian reaching for him. When Trevor glanced from their hands to Sebastian's face, he found an expression so measured as to be unreadable. Impossible to tell if this gesture was intended to give reassurance or simply maintain their facade, though the steadiness of Sebastian's gaze suggested he recognized some hint of Trevor's inner turmoil.

The touch eased the worst of his tension. It felt so comfortable and *right*, despite the strange pretext of the evening. Trevor drew a slow breath to collect himself, then turned his hand over to interlace their fingers.

He averted his eyes as he did so. Pretending to direct his attention to the wedding party but in fact blatantly hiding. His face would be too honest if he held eye contact. He couldn't afford to let his expression give away all his secrets. If Sebastian noticed how much Trevor enjoyed having him close, he might ask the wrong questions.

Better to maintain the illusion that he was unaffected. With any luck, Sebastian wouldn't find it strange for him to stare a little too hard at the smiling brides.

When the toasts finally ended, dinner was served with remarkable efficiency. Trevor was too much on edge to appreciate or notice the meal. His stomach fluttered at unpredictable intervals, and his pulse sped every damn time Sebastian smiled at him.

From his other side, his best friend continued to emanate unfettered incredulity. Cam wouldn't call him out in front of witnesses, but Trevor could feel the hard stare drilling into him. He avoided eye contact and tried to finish more of his dinner, grateful Sebastian was such a charmer. Trevor was too distracted to keep his end of the table conversation lively, but thanks to his date, there were no awkward lulls, no agonizing silences, no floundering for new subjects. Sebastian directed the meandering stream of topics with a deft and subtle hand, always asking exactly the right question to manage a timely detour.

Trevor had seen Sebastian maneuver this way plenty of times before. He knew it was a skill both delicate and meticulously practiced, honed through years in a field that required endless diplomacy. The results were impressive, and holy fuck, did he owe a favor or six for this performance.

As people gradually began scattering from the table, Trevor breathed easier. A contradictory mix of nerves and satisfaction crept through him as he and Sebastian also rose to make a circuit of the enormous lawn. He felt surprisingly at ease with his arm around Sebastian's waist and with Sebastian's arm draped across his shoulders in return.

Here, too, he envied Sebastian's casual eloquence. Trevor could turn a clever phrase in a courtroom, but social settings always undid him. Tonight, it didn't matter if he was terrible at making small talk. With

Sebastian on his arm, the pressure to make an immediate good impression fell away. Sebastian's graceful charm cushioned both of them, and Trevor could calm down and be himself.

Networking at professional functions would be so much more enjoyable if he could attend them like this. Half of a team, playing off one another's strengths. For a fleeting instant, he wondered if he could convince Sebastian to give this fake-dating experiment a lengthier exploration.

He dismissed the thought the second it entered his mind, but with a definite whiff of wistfulness. It would be nice—a small fraction as nice as it would be to date Sebastian for real, though he had no excuse for entertaining such an idea.

The sprawling green yard was already full of guests. Together, Trevor and Sebastian passed the stone steps of the church, the open bar in the corner of the lawn, the wall of high bushes edging the night-dark garden beyond. Distracted by fantasies of future nights with Sebastian on his arm, Trevor didn't notice until too late that they had been drawn into the inescapable orbit of Emma's parents.

The couple was every bit as stiff and condescending as he remembered. Caroline gave him a plastic smile while watching him through narrowed eyes. Phillip shook his hand with crushing strength as though trying to make Trevor flinch. Trevor was used to it—braced for it—which meant he could hold his ground and offer a convincing veneer of courtesy that the pair frankly did not deserve.

The Calcaterras showed a sliver of pleased recognition at being introduced to Sebastian, though their practiced smiles did a poor job of masking their critical curiosity. Once upon a very long time ago, Trevor might have doubted his perceptions. After all, no one in Emma's family had ever said a rude word directly to his face.

But he had dated Emma for four years. He'd had plenty of opportunities to eavesdrop and confirm their pretentious attitudes didn't jibe with their daughter's warm heart.

With Sebastian beside him, it was easier to meet those ice-thin smiles with measured politeness. He could tell himself it didn't matter whether these assholes saw his worth, and more importantly, he could believe it. He was here on his own terms.

He had nothing to prove.

Trevor must have drifted too far into his own head because he was startled by a sudden interjection, Sebastian's voice rising to stall the conversation.

"Oh! This is our song. Please excuse us; it's been lovely chatting with you but—" Sebastian paused, withdrawing his arm from across Trevor's shoulders and taking his hand instead. "Dance with me?"

Trevor grinned and squeezed Sebastian's hand. He didn't recognize the song that had started playing. It was too sedate for his taste, ideal for a slow dance. Perfect for the timely fiction Sebastian had just manufactured, transforming what should have been a rude interruption into an unimpeachable romantic gesture.

When Sebastian responded to Trevor's wordless reaction by raising their joined hands and pressing a kiss to the inside of his wrist, it took all of Trevor's self-control to keep his legs from buckling.

He hoped he didn't sound too breathless when he finally managed to answer, "I'd love to dance."

*

As he followed Sebastian across the lawn, it occurred to Trevor that it was probably a good thing he didn't know this song. Whatever the hell it was, he would never be able to listen to it again without being drawn back to this stupid, pining, heartsick moment.

Sebastian led the way onto the dance floor, already crowded with couples. He hadn't let go of Trevor's hand, and he tugged now, pulling their bodies close and circling Trevor's waist with one arm, apparently perfectly comfortable with the way Trevor snugged close to reciprocate.

Maybe guilt would come later. Though the gesture was freely offered, Trevor relished it in ways he had no right to. Sebastian couldn't know what this simple dance—not to mention the rest of tonight's deceptively casual intimacy—was doing to him. Trevor's pulse pounded fast and hard, his every sense flashing alert. Sebastian's arms held strong and warm around him, and God, Sebastian was so *tall*. Trevor had never in his life felt quite so small and protected.

Returning to reality tomorrow would crush him. He needed to start bracing for the letdown now.

Instead, he tucked his head under Sebastian's chin, leaning into the broad chest and the thump-thump-thumping heartbeat. Sebastian's pulse was speeding nearly as fast as Trevor's. They weren't so much dancing as swaying. This might even be a different song, for all Trevor knew. He couldn't pay attention to the music when his arms and senses were full of Sebastian Greer.

Drifting so helplessly in the moment, Trevor almost didn't hear the low question Sebastian murmured in his ear.

"Are you okay?" The words were carried on a soft rumble that made Trevor's chest ache.

"Yeah. Thanks for getting us out of there." Trevor reluctantly straightened, easing back from the embrace he hadn't meant to fall quite so far into. He blushed a little as he raised his head, trying not to broadcast too obviously how much he wanted to keep cuddling into Sebastian's arms. "Thanks for all of this. For being here. I don't know how I'll ever return the favor."

Sebastian's eyes held a flicker of unfamiliar intensity. "You don't owe me anything. I wanted to be here."

"Why?" The word came out shaky and rough. Suddenly the eye contact between them felt overwhelming, but he couldn't look away.

They weren't dancing anymore. Hell, they weren't even moving. They had stopped completely, standing together near the edge of the dance floor as one song ended and a faster one began.

The force of Sebastian's focus made it difficult to breathe. Trevor couldn't speak, couldn't think, couldn't bring himself to let go. In a single breathless moment, his entire body lit with irrational hope, shivering in Sebastian's arms. Except for a subtle trembling in Trevor's limbs, the stillness was complete. He and Sebastian stood in a perfect bubble of private reality, heedless of the other wedding guests surrounding them on all sides.

The night shifted and fractured around him when Sebastian raised a hand to Trevor's face. Fingertips ghosted against his cheek in an impossibly light touch, faint warmth, and a hint of question. Then Sebastian's palm curled along his jawline. Still soft. Still tentative. Guiding him to raise his face and holding him with riveted attention.

This couldn't be part of their ruse. No one was paying any damn attention to them, lost in the otherwise lively dance floor. There was no audience to pretend for. Just the two of them, practically anonymous in a sea of bodies undulating and jumping to the music.

Sebastian leaned closer, gaze dropping to Trevor's mouth.

Oh God. Sebastian was going to kiss him.

Trevor caught and held his breath, terrified of somehow altering their unexpected course.

But the kiss didn't come. Instead, the guiding hands fell away. Sebastian took a single backward step, letting go of Trevor and withdrawing as though behind a brick wall. His expression shuttered, and Trevor suddenly couldn't read anything past the blank set of his features.

Trevor knew this face. He had seen the same measured air in courtrooms and judges' chambers a hundred times. Moments of caution. Guarded reactions. It hurt to see the sharp intensity of a few seconds ago evaporate so abruptly.

A lump of disappointment rose in his throat, and he struggled to banish the sense of rejection. A hard swallow barely restrained the immediate urge to ask what was wrong. There was no point asking why Sebastian had stopped—Trevor must have misread the signals. Why should he feel utterly dejected at not receiving a kiss he'd had no rational grounds to expect?

Worse, if he'd done something to make Sebastian uncomfortable, the last thing either of them needed was to spotlight the misstep and linger over the misunderstanding. He couldn't even blame alcohol. Neither of them had consumed so much as a drop through dinner, too focused on their deception to visit the open bar.

Before Trevor could find words to break the impasse, Sebastian said, "Are you all right alone for a few minutes? I need to find a restroom."

As excuses went, this one was perfectly reasonable. Trevor might have believed it under different circumstances. But he couldn't take the request at face value now. Not after whatever had just happened—or more accurately *hadn't* happened—between them.

He nodded numbly. "Sure. I'll meet you at the table later. We can leave whenever you want." He hadn't spoken directly to either of the brides since the reception line, but Emma would forgive him for any perceived slight.

He stepped off the dance floor, careful to not watch Sebastian flee. He refused to let anyone see him looking as smitten and pathetic as he inevitably would if he tracked Sebastian's progress across the grass. His heart was already a pulp of disappointment, and his ego couldn't take the extra hit.

As he deliberately averted his gaze, he spotted both brides moving directly toward him. They seemed simultaneously exhausted and euphoric, and as they drew closer, their smiles glowed bright and sincere. Like the corona of the sun, the fervency of so much happiness was impossible to look at straight on.

Emma moved right in, scooping him into a crushing hug. "I wasn't sure you'd stay."

Sloane held back a little, but her smile spread at the sight of Trevor's flustered attempt to return the unexpected hug. He probably squeezed too tightly and withdrew too fast, but he couldn't help it. Never mind the frantic tumult twisting inside him. He couldn't begin to guess at proper etiquette for hugging the ex-girlfriend who insisted on remaining friends. He hoped they might find their footing one day. But in the meantime, there was no denying the awkwardness of his place here.

Trevor found a smile for Emma. "Of course I stayed. I wouldn't miss your party."

He forced himself to ignore the swoop in his stomach and the way his entire body ached to turn and search for Sebastian in the crowd.

Chapter Five

Thankfully, it only took a few minutes for a swarm of other guests to draw the newlyweds onto the dance floor. Emma shot Trevor an apologetic glance as she was pulled away, and he absolved her with a jaunty wave. She didn't need to know how relieved he was to be left alone. The current state of Trevor's heart had nothing to do with her.

As Sloane and Emma vanished amid the enthusiastic crowd of dancers, Trevor let out a quiet sigh and dropped the facade.

Alone despite the noisy throng, Trevor reminded himself it was getting late. Now that he had actually talked to Emma, no one would bat an eye at him calling it a night. A glance at their table told him Sebastian hadn't yet returned. Trevor could send a text to check in, but it hadn't been all that long since Sebastian's retreat. Basic politeness demanded he wait at least a few more minutes before nagging his date to take him home.

Nearby stood a noisy, jovially inebriated cluster of vaguely familiar people. Some wore the matching maroon of the wedding party and still looked remarkably done up. Others had shed ties and shoes and jackets, crumbling toward casual disarray with the lengthening night. Cam stood among them, arguing animatedly with one of the groomsmen about something Trevor couldn't decipher from a distance. It would only be a matter of time before one of them glanced over and spotted him. So, Trevor did what any reasonable, clever, emotionally exhausted partygoer would do.

He made a break for the gardens, ducking between tall hedges and away from the exuberant chaos.

Several seconds passed before his eyes adjusted from warm reception lighting to the comparative darkness of moon and starlight. The noise of the party echoed high and boisterous behind him, but the path beyond the first row of bushes felt surprisingly peaceful. Flowers tangled everywhere, their petals white and gray in the darkness. They gave off an inviting aroma as he edged farther along the gravel path.

Away from the music.

Toward a few minutes' solitude.

He moved without purpose or conscious direction, no desire in his head beyond putting as much distance as possible between himself and the churchyard. His phone remained in his pocket, silent, but sure to alert him if Sebastian texted. And the garden seemed extensive but not especially labyrinthine. He should have no trouble retracing his steps as soon as he'd satisfied this itch to isolate.

He needed to get his wayward heart under control before he faced Sebastian for the drive home.

A murmur of voices ahead reached him so softly that he'd drawn surprisingly close by the time he noticed the conversation over the music echoing behind him. The voices grew more distinct with every step, until Trevor rounded a tall corner shrub and startled to a halt. In a small clearing directly ahead of him, illuminated in faint gold by a single wispy lamppost, Sebastian and Josiah Greer stood glaring at each other.

Rather, Sebastian was glaring. Josiah wore an air of brotherly disapproval that Trevor recognized as a universal constant. His own siblings had used the same look on him hundreds of times. Even on an unfamiliar face obscured by shadows, Trevor could recognize the nuance of it.

"—don't have to justify myself to you," Sebastian finished with a marked rise in volume. Judging from the way he didn't bother to check himself, he had no idea he and Josiah were no longer alone.

"Of course you don't." The dry edge of Josiah's tone matched perfectly the expression on his face.

"I have no intention of expressing any of this to him," Sebastian said.

"Why not?" This time, Josiah sounded sincerely perplexed.

The emotion that crossed Sebastian's face in answer was so raw it made Trevor's heart hurt. "It would be a breach of trust."

"Worse than taking advantage of an awkward social situation to get close to a man you can't be honest with?"

Trevor's breath hitched so hard he couldn't believe the two didn't hear him. But engrossed as they were in their conversation, neither so much as turned in his direction. Sebastian's eyes flashed wide, and his jaw dropped. He stared at Josiah as though his brother had kicked him in the stomach. Trevor knew he should leave. This conversation wasn't his to witness. But it was about him, damn it. It must be. And he wasn't strong enough to walk away now.

An agonized eon passed with no answer to Josiah's accusation. Trevor waited with desperate, guilt-tinged impatience, holding his breath as long as possible.

At last, Sebastian recovered some semblance of composure. "My interest in him is completely inappropriate. Our professional relationship—"

"Ended years ago," Josiah said with steely precision.

"He still considers me a mentor. How can I jeopardize our friendship when he's given no indication of wanting more?"

Trevor's heart lurched with a hungry feeling, even as Josiah barked an incredulous laugh. "*No indication*? Jesus,

Sebastian, have you been at this party tonight?"

"Tonight is not representative of Trevor's feelings."

Again, Trevor's chest tightened with wild hope. There was no possibility of mistake now. This wasn't assumption and supposition. Wishful thinking couldn't be tinting his perceptions. Sebastian had said his name, and there was no taking it back.

"Really?" Josiah pressed, unrelenting. "Because I saw you two on that dance floor. You were going to kiss him, and he was clearly going to let you."

Sebastian's eyes closed, and his entire posture tensed. "Josiah, please. I know you're trying to help. But stop. Just. Stop."

Silence, sharp and painful, ricocheted through the garden for several seconds.

Then, so softly Trevor strained to hear him, Josiah said, "You can't keep doing this to yourself. You've been in love with him too long."

A sound somewhere between a gasp and a squeak filled the clearing. When Sebastian and Josiah both snapped their gazes toward him, Trevor realized it must have come from him.

He stood frozen, too guilty to pretend he hadn't been eavesdropping. He knew damn well he shouldn't be here. He sure as hell shouldn't have overheard the impossible words Josiah had breathed into the night. The caught-out horror spreading across Sebastian's face made Trevor feel like a complete asshole as he stepped fully into the clearing.

A gleeful wave crested inside him, fast and torrential and undercutting any sliver of remorse. Fuck it, nothing about this was a disaster. Trevor shouldn't have learned the truth this way, but he had no desire to go back now. He needed to find the right words to move forward. He needed to impart his own confession before Sebastian had a chance to recant.

As he drew near, he tore his gaze from Sebastian's stunned and handsome face to look directly at Josiah. "Can we have a minute?"

"Have as many minutes as you want." Josiah maintained a neutral tone, but a subtle glint of smugness flashed in his eyes. A moment later, he vanished into the shadows, so quick and smooth it could have been humorous under less fraught circumstances.

Trevor's heart continued to pound so hard he felt lightheaded. But before he could speak, Sebastian turned aside, gaze directed deliberately elsewhere.

"I'm sorry," Sebastian said.

Surely Trevor could blame his spinning senses for the thoughtless way he blurted, "For being in love with me?"

Sebastian flinched at the blunt question, but he also stood straighter. Sudden, perfect posture. In profile, his sharp expression was easy to read despite scant light and heavy shadows.

"No," Sebastian said, but continued before Trevor's heart could finish sinking in disappointment. "I won't apologize for that. I'm sorry for misleading you tonight. I shouldn't have accepted your invitation."

"Sebastian—"

"These false pretenses were unconscionable. Josiah's right. I took advantage of the situation."

The giddy sensation rose once more in Trevor's chest, and he retorted without thinking. "You and me both."

Sebastian pivoted toward him and stared as though Trevor had sprouted wings.

The knee-jerk instinct to echo the apology was a powerful one. Trevor knew he'd fucked up, plain and simple. But he also owed his companion an explanation. Sebastian stood there staring at him, gorgeous face slack with shock, watchful eyes glinting in the golden lamplight.

Sebastian looked very much like he was holding his breath, like he couldn't guess where all this was going, like he didn't dare to hope.

Trevor knew the feeling.

With difficulty he kept his voice steady. "Okay, screw it. Cards on the table. I shouldn't have asked you to be my fake boyfriend tonight. It was manipulative and shitty, considering I've been fucked up over you for years."

Sebastian's eyes widened, which should have been impossible considering how floored he already looked. "What...are you saying?"

A long breath, slow and deep, grounded Trevor enough to continue. "I'm saying I'm sorry. Because I've been dishonest too." He eased forward across the narrow distance separating them. Cautious. Stopping just outside of touching range, though all he wanted was to grab Sebastian and hold on like both their lives depended on it. "But if you really are in love with me, maybe we can skip the apology feedback loop and do something productive about it."

No trace of Trevor's usual bravado reached the quiet words, anxious as he was to get this right. Sebastian had thoroughly confirmed everything he so desperately wanted to be true. After years of paying excessive attention, Trevor wondered how he could have failed to notice Sebastian watching him back.

"Something productive?" Sebastian echoed, his tone incredulous and intrigued.

"Were you really going to kiss me back there?" Trevor tilted his head in the direction of the reception and the dance floor.

"Yes."

"Will you kiss me now?" The question felt momentous. It felt eager and impossible and urgent. All his years of unrequited pining, abruptly unwinding from their hopeless tangle around Trevor's heart.

Silence held endlessly as they watched each other. Then, without another word, Sebastian took a single step forward. The party buzzed at the edge of Trevor's awareness, faint through the heavy thudding of his own pulse in his ears. He breathed a startled but delighted gasp when broad hands framed his face. It was a gentle touch. Warm strength measured into something soft as Sebastian guided Trevor's head back, seeking eye contact.

Holding him like a question.

"Don't tease," Trevor begged, voice low as a whisper. "God, please don't tease me." He'd imagined this so many times, and he doubted he would ever recover if Sebastian changed course again. The night had settled calm and perfect around them, making the cool air and empty garden a whole separate world from the wedding reception. Golden lamplight mixed faintly with the cool blue glow of the moon.

Sebastian leaned down, his breath ghosting across Trevor's skin, warmth shining in his dark eyes. Trevor closed his eyes and covered Sebastian's hands with his own. Accepting, encouraging, bracing himself to rise onto his toes if that was what it took to get what he wanted.

"—could've sworn I saw him disappear this way. Trevor?" Cam's voice cut through the garden, shredding the peaceful moment in an instant.

Trevor stood rooted in place, but he couldn't prevent Sebastian from jerking back and away. He recognized the retreat for the panicked instinct it was—putting safe distance between them though they were doing nothing wrong.

He turned toward the now unmistakable clamor of a small group approaching. The gaggle emerged from behind a stand of decorative trees with Cam at the vanguard, moving a little unsteadily. The handful of people following looked equally wobbly, much the same as they had when Trevor spotted them outside the garden. Now, they ran a blurry range from tipsy to outright drunk. Some of them leaned on each other, laughing as they followed Cam's lead.

Trevor didn't begrudge them their good time. Considering Emma and Sloane's cautious natures, there would be plenty of sober cabs lined up to get everyone home in one piece. But he resented the hell out of the interruption, and it took all his self-restraint to bite back an unkind greeting.

When Cam spotted Trevor, a wide grin spread across his face. "There you are!" He gestured toward the bridesmaid immediately to his left. "Mia requested your favorite song from the DJ, and then you weren't there. So I said we should find you and try again. You gonna come to the dance floor or what?" Cam's gaze darted to the space directly behind Trevor, where Sebastian's warmth radiated despite the interruption, and a first flicker of confusion narrowed his eyes.

Normally, Trevor enjoyed the scatterbrained version of his friend who emerged after a couple of stiff cocktails. He had no idea who Mia was beyond the dress putting her amid the wedding party, but Cam's habit of making instant friends was nothing new. Certainly, Cam's cheerful exuberance made him fun to drink with. It was nice to have an extrovert around to keep things noisy.

But tonight, Trevor wanted to kick Cam in the shins and tell him to fuck off.

He settled for a clipped, "I'm busy right now. I'll find you later."

"But—" Mia tried to chime in, peering at him through elegantly curled bangs. Trevor locked her with a hard stare before she could finish, and the expression must have been uncharacteristically fierce. She stopped talking and closed her mouth with an audible click.

"I'm. Busy." He gritted the repetition through clenched teeth. When he glanced once more at Cam, he found perplexity meeting his stare as Cam's gaze darted back and forth between Trevor and Sebastian.

Trevor was already bracing to snark the interlopers into submission, little as he cherished the wasted time.

But a second later, comprehension reached Cam's eyes, and he turned to redirect the group. "Forget it, guys. The DJ won't play the same song twice anyway. Let's go back to the party." Cam's demeanor was no steadier than before, but he exuded all the solidity necessary to guide the confused cluster of onlookers. No explanations, no personal revelations, just an easy nudging back the way they'd come. As he directed everyone away, Cam turned to throw one final glance over his shoulder, but Trevor wouldn't try to answer his unspoken questions before finishing this conversation.

"Trevor?" Sebastian eased closer as the garden finally emptied around them.

Trevor breathed a low, exasperated exhale and shook his head.

"Fuck this. Come on." He grabbed Sebastian's hand and tugged, following the gravel path deeper into the garden. He didn't know how far they could travel, but he wanted all the space he could put between them and any possible intrusions. They needed somewhere private—somewhere they wouldn't be interrupted—amid moonlit paths and plants.

He didn't stop until he and Sebastian were truly alone.

The place was less a clearing than a narrow corridor of mown grass. Flower-covered bushes towered to either side of the crevice. A bench sat partially obscured in a heavy swathe of shadow. Perfect. Trevor guided Sebastian in front of the bench and gave a commanding push.

In the silvery light of the moon, Sebastian's smile was radiant as he followed the wordless instruction and sat down. Then, every movement smooth, he spread out like the whole damn bench belonged to him. His long legs stretched across the grass in a deliberate sprawl as he draped both arms along the back of the bench. He slouched invitingly, peering up into Trevor's face with a subtle glint of mischief.

The pose looked so enticing Trevor almost whimpered. Then, slow and graceful, Sebastian smiled and quirked a single eyebrow at him.

Trevor's heart melted, and he breathed an eager sound—more choked moan than whimper—as he dropped to his knees astride Sebastian's lap and kissed him with all the finesse of a freight train.

Sebastian laughed into the kiss, and the fond rumble of amusement made Trevor's toes curl right there in his shoes. He twined his arms around Sebastian's broad shoulders, shivering at the sensation of fingers grazing his scalp. Then Sebastian wrapped him up tight, powerful arms holding him, as Sebastian returned the kiss so enthusiastically Trevor thought he might cry.

This couldn't be real. In all his unrequited fantasies, Trevor had never harbored a scrap of delusion about one day getting what he wanted.

He drew back reluctantly and only in deference to the inevitable need for oxygen. He was breathing hard, but so was Sebastian. When Trevor opened his eyes, it surprised him to discover how clearly he could read Sebastian's face. The smile was back, amazed and pleased. Emotion glittered in eyes that looked like ebony in the dark garden.

"We should probably talk about this," Sebastian noted, though his tone was sunny. His hands settled low on Trevor's hips, beneath the black suit jacket. Gentle fingertips brushed the small of Trevor's back through his shirt.

The layers of fancy dress abruptly weighed stiflingly on him. Trevor's shirt collar threatened to choke him, his tie cinched too tight. He ached to be somewhere with walls and doors and locks. Somewhere he could keep right on touching Sebastian in all the greedy ways he craved.

"Talking is overrated," he retorted and grinned when the observation earned a wry chuckle.

But instead of kissing him again, Sebastian peered searchingly into his face. The smile fell away in favor of a more serious aspect—the kind of watchful attention that made Trevor feel like all his secrets were on display. He met the look without flinching, even as he resisted the urge to squirm beneath the scrutiny.

"What do you want, Trevor?" Sebastian asked. "Tonight. Tomorrow. Where do we go from here?" His low tone carried a complicated swirl of hope-hesitation-fondness-desire.

Trevor considered his answer with more care than he had ever exercised in his entire thoughtfully planned life. "I want to go back out there to tell Cam and your brother we're not pretending anymore."

Sebastian's breath caught audibly. "Yeah?"

"Yeah." An unstoppable smile spread across Trevor's face, and feverish giddiness rolled through him. "I want to spend what's left of this party making up for lost time. And then I want you to take me home. Your place or mine, I don't care which, as long as we go there together."

"Mmm." Sebastian let go of his hips and wrapped his arms around Trevor's waist, pulling him forward and crushing him close. "And tomorrow?"

Tomorrow was Sunday, thank God. "Tomorrow we sleep in and cuddle all day. Then maybe I take you to dinner?" Trevor didn't know precisely how this was going to work. How should he go about courting someone after obsessing over them for years, especially when that someone had apparently wanted him back the entire time? How would they structure an actual relationship into their busy lives?

How could he pretend to set a reasonable pace when he was already in over his head?

"Dinner sounds lovely," Sebastian declared. "All of what you said sounds lovely."

Then he kissed Trevor again, and for a while, neither of them said anything at all.

*

By the time they returned to the reception, the crowd was beginning to quiet. The dance floor stood empty. Guests were sobering up and going home. Cam, in particular, looking lucid and clear even from a distance, seemed to have collected himself and switched over to water.

For all Trevor's desire to make an absolute spectacle of himself with Sebastian, he was glad they'd ducked into a washroom and set themselves to rights before rejoining the festivities. He wanted to proclaim his new revelations to the world, but some details were too personal to broadcast widely.

For a moment, he feared he would have to find some clever ruse to break his best friend off from the pack. If he made a thing of it, people might wonder what he couldn't share with the rest of the dwindling group Cam had attached himself to. Strictly speaking, Trevor's explanations could wait. There was no reason he needed to update Cam tonight. But a twist of disappointment pulsed in his chest at the thought of leaving this unfinished business behind him.

Awkward as this conversation promised to be, he wanted Cam to know tonight's amended truth.

Before Trevor could decide whether to barge into the group or give up on the idea, Cam raised his head and glanced over. Peeling away from the flock, he headed straight for them.

"Can I talk to you a minute?" Cam asked when he got close enough to keep his voice down. His eyes flicked to Sebastian, not unfriendly but not subtle either. "Alone?"

"Take your time," Sebastian said with an intensity Trevor couldn't decipher until he added, "I think I see my brother near the bar."

Oh. Trevor grinned widely as he realized Sebastian was giving him exactly what he'd asked for back in that secluded patch of garden. This was a perfectly crafted chance for both Cam and Josiah to learn simultaneously there was no more charade. And then Sebastian would drive him home, hopefully to do a whole lot more than make out on a park bench. Excitement zinged through Trevor's blood.

"Okay."

It was ridiculous how much audible delight glittered in those two syllables, but Trevor didn't care. He couldn't find so much as a scrap of sheepishness as Cam glanced back and forth between them in obvious confusion. Trevor's smile stretched wider, shameless, and he turned away from Cam just long enough to rise onto his toes and kiss Sebastian on the cheek. Only then did he follow Cam away from the thinning crowd, around a corner of the church and completely out of sight.

The instant they were alone, Cam whirled on him. "Trevor, what the *actual hell?"*

Cam's frantic exasperation ought to have made Trevor feel at least a little guilty, but he couldn't seem to turn down the wattage of his luminous grin.

"You said he wasn't your boyfriend." Cam gestured behind them with this reminder, though Sebastian and the reception weren't visible from their current vantage point.

"He wasn't."

"Oh, but he is now?" Cam didn't seem the least bit placated.

Trevor definitely shouldn't be this amused at his best friend's expense. "Yes." He shrugged. "You *did* ask why he agreed to come to the wedding."

"You— He— How the *fuck*?"

"Just lucky, I guess."

"Lucky," Cam echoed, incredulous. With incremental slowness, some of the disbelief began to fade. "You are completely impossible."

"You didn't tell anyone the truth, did you? About the whole not-really-my-boyfriend thing?" Prepared as he'd been to admit the truth eventually, Trevor didn't relish the idea of treading the ground multiple times to convince the world this time was for real. *No, really. Seriously. We're actually dating this time; it's true, I promise.*

"Of course I didn't tell anyone." Cam rolled his eyes. "That's your mess, not mine."

But it wasn't a mess. It was glorious, and Trevor couldn't stop grinning. All those people who had met Sebastian as his charming plus-one tonight—who already thought they were together—could simply carry on knowing. He could let those first impressions stand.

"Okay. Wow." Cam shook his head as though clearing it, then blinked at Trevor with steady curiosity. "So. What now?"

Trevor didn't have a succinct answer. He couldn't be as blunt or as candid with Cam as he'd been with Sebastian. But he clapped his friend on the shoulder with a shrug and dragged him back around the corner.

By the time Trevor and Sebastian made it to the car, the clock on the dashboard read nearly two in the morning. Trevor felt wide awake despite the late hour, vibrating with unrestrained energy as he climbed into the passenger seat.

He buckled in and waited, expecting the engine to turn over and start. When it didn't, he turned to his companion. Sebastian sat in the driver's seat, perfectly relaxed, one hand on the wheel. His entire focus fixed on Trevor as if he was trying to process their new reality.

Trevor knew the feeling. "Everything okay?" he asked anyway.

"Of course." A lovely little smile quirked at the corner of Sebastian's mouth. "Just enjoying the view."

Trevor blushed, a thrill rushing through him at the compliment. He suddenly wanted to unbuckle his seatbelt and crawl across the center console into Sebastian's lap. At the very least, he wanted to get loose so he could claim a pleading kiss. His lips tingled from all those kisses in the garden, but they weren't enough. He could never have enough.

With difficulty, he stayed in his seat because, even more, he wanted to get home. Why linger in a dark, empty parking lot when they could be comfortably indoors, at liberty to do anything they pleased?

These were the thoughts swirling through his head as the car finally started, engine rumbling soothingly in the quiet. Trevor reached out and covered Sebastian's hand atop the stick shift.

"Home?" he asked.

"Home," Sebastian agreed and put the car in gear.

Chapter Six

The grating shrill of his alarm clock knocked Trevor out of sleep and into awareness of the predawn morning. Muddled and half tangled in a dubious dream—about butterflies and secret underground tunnels—he was lucid enough to experience a pang of irritation at his past self for forgetting to turn the damn thing off. The weekend was for sleeping in. He always did extra work for his endless caseload on his days off, but that was no reason to wake up before the sun had finished rising.

He muttered a string of indistinct curses and, without bothering to open his eyes, reached back to swat in the general direction of the snooze button.

"Ow," came a distinctly amused protest when Trevor's hand smacked into something far too warm and soft to be his nightstand.

A shoulder. A *bare* shoulder. To go with *Sebastian Greer's voice*, rumbling low and lovely behind him.

Trevor snapped his eyes open. In the span of a heartbeat, he came fully alert, and his senses spun at the whiplash of it. On the floor lay the components of his discarded tuxedo, while Sebastian's outfit had been folded meticulously over a chair. The edge of the bed was closer than usual in his line of sight. Of course it was. He lay on his side well over from the middle of the mattress where he usually slept, thanks to the inferno sharing the bed with him.

A big, welcome, affectionate inferno. Snugged right along Trevor's back, between him and the alarm clock, which was still ringing rudely through the room.

He could ask Sebastian to kill the alarm, but instead, Trevor squirmed onto his back, then all the way over onto his other side. He braced one arm beneath him to stretch up and over his guest and switch the alarm off. Yes, it gave him a chance to appreciate the unaccustomed bulk of a second person in his bed, and yes, it let him slide along Sebastian's very naked form in all kinds of unnecessary ways. But surely, it was also more practical than trying to explain the alarm clock buttons.

He could almost convince himself of this, right up to the moment he saw Sebastian's expression below him.

A smile. But somehow, the word *smile* didn't quite encompass the swathe of emotion softening Sebastian's face. The curl at both corners of his mouth edged higher as he caught Trevor looking, unvarnished affection reflected in the subtle movement. Crow's-feet creased the edges of eyes so deep and lovely Trevor could easily get lost in them. Brown cheeks honest-to-God *dimpled* in the gray light sneaking between window curtains, and a fleeting glimpse of teeth flashed behind full lips.

Trevor froze in place. He couldn't help it. His next move would have been to pull away and settle back down, but he couldn't bear to withdraw.

"Good morning," he said, not particularly caring if he sounded flustered. He was vividly aware of his own nakedness, of all the casual yet intimate places he and Sebastian were touching. His entire body warmed, and he couldn't decide whether the emotional or the physical wanting was more overwhelming.

Despite their mutual desperation, they hadn't actually done anything last night. Trevor's burst of energy hadn't lasted even half the drive home before the adrenaline crash knocked him flat. Between the two of them, they'd barely managed to strip down and crawl beneath the covers. Hell, Trevor couldn't remember finding an extra pillow for Sebastian—though he must have done so in a half-asleep haze because there were two pillows on the bed.

Sebastian's smile deepened, and he reached up to trace wondering fingertips along Trevor's face. The touch ghosted along cheekbones, jaw, throat. Endearingly tentative.

"Good mor—" Sebastian *oofed* into something suspiciously like laughter when Trevor interrupted him with a kiss.

Trevor didn't care if Sebastian was laughing at him. He only cared that the touch slid back as Sebastian cupped the nape of his neck and tugged him closer. Sebastian's body shifted against him—beneath him—and Sebastian's free arm slipped around his waist. Trevor allowed himself to be pulled and maneuvered, guided into a straddle across broad hips as the kiss turned filthy between them.

He breathed a needy hum around an especially insistent thrust of tongue. Then Trevor pressed one hand over Sebastian's pounding heart and slid the other to cup his jaw in order to kiss him all the harder.

Fucking hell, he couldn't believe this was real. Sebastian here. Sebastian touching him. Sebastian *naked in his bed.* Through every wild fantasy Trevor had ever entertained, it never once occurred to him this might actually happen. He savored the moment. Such satisfaction was not to be squandered now that they were here.

Eventually, they needed to break apart, if only for the sake of oxygen. The rapid rise and fall of Sebastian's chest matched his own, and Trevor's breath turned shallow with longing. His body flushed hot, despite his nakedness and the fact that the thin sheet had fallen completely away.

He was also deliciously aware of the stiff nudge of Sebastian's erection, equal parts teasing and hungry. The stuttery little movements of Sebastian's hips held no urgency, but there was also no mistaking the heated intent.

Trevor's breath caught. His own dick had stiffened, equally insistent, and he hoped they were about to do something about it.

Together.

When at last he regained enough self-control to open his eyes, he found Sebastian watching him with unprecedented intensity.

"Are you all right?" Sebastian's tone was easier to decipher than the complicated amalgam of emotions written across his face. The syllables echoed with an undercurrent of fondness, a singe of desire, a hum of eager anticipation. All of this accompanied by a shiver of incredulity, as though Sebastian also couldn't entirely believe he'd woken in Trevor's bed.

“I’m good.” Trevor ground his body slowly—teasingly—deliberately down against the hard-on pressing between his legs. “Great. Superb. Perfect. I have literally never been better.”

Sebastian’s eyes fluttered shut, his face flushing as a groan escaped in answer. Trevor could have whimpered his delight. He meant the words with painful sincerity. Wracking his brain and actively trying to come up with memories of ever being happier than this, he couldn’t find anything. Not even Emma had brought him to this improbable threshold, and he boggled at the revelation.

Sebastian blinked and opened his eyes with apparent difficulty. Both of his hands settled at Trevor’s hips, stilling the slow rocking where their bodies met.

With equal difficulty, Trevor forced a slower breath into his lungs. “Do you want me to stop?”

"No." Sebastian rolled his hips upward as though to emphasize the point, jostling Trevor's weight and creating unbearable friction.

The shock of pleasure careened along Trevor's entire nervous system, and he caught his lower lip between his teeth to keep from moaning aloud. He scraped a handful of brain cells together as he arched atop Sebastian.

"I should probably warn you; I don't have anything we need for more...ambitious activities."

Sebastian grunted a startled laugh and thrust upward once more. Between the two of them, precome was already rendering their movements slick, turning their rhythm filthier and clumsier by the second.

"You are an impossible man," Sebastian murmured, the words carrying a subtle but incendiary chuckle. "How can you make *fucking* sound like a matter of decorum and procedure?"

Trevor grinned, wild and unapologetic. "I'm an attorney."

With startling efficiency, Sebastian surged under him. Between the strength in broad hands and the burst of motion, Trevor was not surprised to find himself on his back. Neither was he surprised Sebastian had put him there or that the trick had been accomplished so easily. Trevor thrilled at the way all that firm weight followed, immediately pinning him to the mattress.

Giddiness filled him at the show of strength. God how he wanted to experience more.

"Never mind more ambitious endeavors," Sebastian said with mischievous levity. "We have all the time in the world for those later. How do you want to get off *now*?"

Trevor's head fell helplessly back as Sebastian punctuated this question with a roll of hips, perfectly aligning their cocks to rub together. Trevor's thighs were still spread wide around Sebastian's waist. The stretch was almost too much as he bent his knees and arched encouragingly beneath the welcome crush of Sebastian's body.

"H-however you like," he managed to answer as desire ricocheted up his spine. "God, as long as you don't stop touching me, you can do whatever the fuck you want."

Sebastian huffed in shivery exasperation, then shook his head. A second later, he dropped forward to nuzzle Trevor's jaw, kiss his throat, nip at his ear.

A brush of lips tickled Trevor's earlobe when Sebastian murmured, "So much for decorum and procedure." A harder bite followed, then a hint of suction at his pulse point. "I *will* need more specific guidance. Tell me what you'd like me to do."

Trevor groaned, low and long. He couldn't remember the last time he'd felt so vulnerable. Sure, he'd had plenty of experience with dirty talk, with begging to be fucked or describing exactly how he wanted to be touched. But somehow, this was overwhelmingly more. A deeper, greedier intimacy caught between his ribs and squeezed his heart, as though he was baring his entire soul rather than discussing the logistics of sex.

Maybe because, for once, he didn't give a fuck about the details. The notion of an orgasm felt abstract and irrelevant in this moment. He didn't need to come, so long as Sebastian kept right on touching him.

But an answer wasn't only expected; it was necessary. As silence extended in the wake of the request, Sebastian fell perfectly and patiently still, making it clear he would only continue once Trevor provided the requested information. When Sebastian eased back, folding one arm to brace himself and make it impossible to avoid eye contact, Trevor had to exert conscious effort to meet the keen attention head-on.

"I honestly don't care," he blurted. It might be the wrong answer, but it was an honest answer, and it was all he had. He forged onward as Sebastian's brow creased. "Your mouth. Your hands. Your knee between my fucking legs. *Anything*. Hell, you could get us both off exactly like this, and it will feel amazing. I'll be happy as long as you stay with me."

Sebastian's eyes widened, absorbing the tidal wave of candor. Trevor continued to meet the piercing stare with all the stubbornness he could muster. He refused to take any of it back.

The considering silence did nothing to quell the desperate arousal coiling inside him.

"You're serious," Sebastian said at last, though he remained maddeningly motionless.

"Christ, of course I am." Trevor didn't mean to sound petulant. He was trying for eloquent, thoughtful, persuasive. So of course, each word came out needier than the last as he admitted, "Look, sex is nice, but it's not my top priority here. I'd like to do all kinds of things with you, but right now, the only thing that feels important is that *you're here*."

He didn't know how else to explain, how to make Sebastian understand. It didn't matter what they chose to do in this moment. Yes, an orgasm would be nice. But far more pressing was the desire to spend all damn morning wrapped in Sebastian's big arms, cuddled and warm and safe.

When Sebastian leaned down to kiss him again, Trevor didn't think he was imagining the undercurrent of understanding. Something considering echoed in the press of lips, the more playful slide of tongue, the teasing nip of teeth. A heartbeat later, the friction of hips nudged forward in perfect time with the thrust of Sebastian's tongue.

This effort without urgency and the lazy momentum rubbing between Trevor's legs suggested they really did understand one another.

"Exactly like this?" Sebastian asked between a string of kisses down the line of Trevor's throat.

"*Yeah.*" Trevor gasped, rolling his hips upward and savoring the resulting zing of pleasure as Sebastian met him halfway. "Yeah, this is good. Oh *fuck*, do that again."

Sebastian obliged and nuzzled under Trevor's jaw. They were both panting now. Somehow, in a handful of heartbeats—or the span of a couple good thrusts—they'd crossed from idle exploration to something urgent after all. Trevor raised his legs to hook his ankles at the small of Sebastian's back. The angle gave him better leverage, and they moved together more surely. Sebastian's cock slid stiff and insistent against his own, trapped between their bodies, and it felt so fucking good.

"*Oh God.*" Sebastian's voice cut through the panting quiet, and then he was gasping Trevor's name in a tone of spilling gravel.

"*Yes.*" The word was all Trevor could manage. His arms wrapped around wide shoulders. He didn't remember putting them there, but he clung to Sebastian as every second carried him closer to the edge. Shaking under the pinning weight, he trailed his own messy kisses along Sebastian's face and neck, tasting the flutter of a rushing pulse.

They orgasmed nearly in unison. Trevor toppled first over the edge, a cry of ecstasy sneaking out like a plea. He grasped desperately at Sebastian's shoulders, clenched his legs, as though the strength of the body on top of him could ground him through any storm.

For another few seconds, Sebastian continued to grind against him. Two more thrusts. Three. And then a sudden jerky stillness as the arms around Trevor tightened and wet heat slicked his stomach alongside the mess he'd already made. Trevor's chest heaved fast and shallow, and he felt amazing.

"Good?" he managed to ask after an absolute eon of trying to catch his breath.

Sebastian snorted and drew back up, meeting his eyes with a glint of amusement. "I don't think 'good' begins to cover it."

"Same," Trevor agreed. Apparently, he had just enough brainpower left for single-syllable words.

When Sebastian kissed him again, Trevor relaxed into the more leisurely satisfaction washing over him. They were both a mess now, and a shower would feel incredible. But for the moment, he didn't care about getting clean. He was too busy drowning in the indulgence of Sebastian's hands and mouth, too caught up in convincing himself he really did get to have this, *keep* this. The quiet intimacy and promise of more. The undeniable warmth of Sebastian Greer, in both his bed and his life.

His entire chest ached in this moment, so full with potential.

"What are you thinking about?" Sebastian placed another quick kiss at the corner of Trevor's mouth.

It was all too much to say out loud, even for a professional talker, so Trevor let the flush of emotion show on his face as he answered blithely, "Breakfast." Those smile lines crinkled at the corners of Sebastian's eyes and made Trevor's heart pulse with ecstatic fondness. "Come on. Shower first, then food." They would have breakfast right back here in bed if he had any say in the matter.

He didn't care if he ended up with crumbs in his sheets, as long as he could spend the entire day wrapped in Sebastian's arms.

*

"There will inevitably be gossip," Sebastian pointed out, though there was no pretense of actual concern in the observation.

Trevor snorted wryly and squirmed back all the tighter against Sebastian's chest. He ignored the sitcom playing on his living room television in favor of this new and infinitely preferable distraction. "If you gave half a damn about gossip, you never would've agreed to be my fake boyfriend last night."

Last night. It boggled his mind that Emma's wedding had been less than twenty-four hours ago, considering the entire foundation of reality had shifted in the interim. It was past noon. Mornings-after tended to be uncomfortable affairs in Trevor's experience, but not this one. He'd never felt more alive in his own skin, and Sebastian had yet to show the faintest inclination to leave. Sure, they were both dressed now, more or less, and only grudgingly. Neither one of them was enough of an asshole to answer the doorbell in a bedsheet—the dude delivering their sandwiches hadn't signed up for that nonsense.

Now, having finished eating, neither of them wanted to move. Trevor's couch was slouchy and comfortable, if not quite deep enough to easily accommodate two grown men. Which meant they were pressed so close they might as well have been occupying the same physical space. Sebastian's front stretched warm and flush all along Trevor's back, his arm folded under Trevor's head like a pillow. Trevor's arm covered the tuck of an embrace around his stomach, and he would never tire of the soft tickle of breath across his neck.

He would never tire of any of this, and he sighed as the quiet pulled and lingered pleasantly between them.

"You're right." Sebastian fluttered the words into a kiss at his nape.

Trevor blinked. It'd been only a short while since he'd spoken, and he'd already lost the entire thread of whatever the hell they'd been talking about.

"Right about what?"

Sebastian choked a short laugh, quickly muffled as he pressed his face to Trevor's shoulder. His mirthful shaking continued for a while, so honest and charming that Trevor didn't mind being a source of amusement. Maybe because there was no hint of mockery in the silent trembling of Sebastian's body. Or maybe because there was something completely thrilling in being able to wring such a reaction out of a usually stern countenance.

It took two full minutes for Sebastian to still and say breathlessly, "You're right that I don't care if people gossip."

"Right." A smile tugged at both corners of Trevor's mouth. "Yes. Exactly. *That's what*

I'm saying." It was technically what he'd forgotten he was saying, but the point stood.

Sebastian fell silent instead of answering, nuzzling at Trevor's shoulder. He held tighter without speaking—a display impossible to decipher without visual cues. Trevor furrowed his brow. The lingering stillness made him want to ask if something was wrong.

If he'd already managed to fuck something up, he needed to know.

Trevor tried to form a follow-up—something serious enough for caution but light enough to avoid ruining the mood—and then Sebastian finally spoke.

"What about you?"

Trevor frowned. "What *about* me?"

"Will the gossip bother you?" A pause, a soft inhale, and then Sebastian continued before Trevor could answer. "I'm not suggesting...I know you won't want to change course regardless. You've made your intentions perfectly clear. But if you're worried about how people will react—"

"I'm not," Trevor interrupted with impatient candor. Then, because he could see the reasons for Sebastian's concern—could understand how things might get complicated for both of them, being together—he forced himself to slow down and address the underlying arguments. "I'll concede the optics aren't great. I used to work for you. I earned my current position based on connections I made in your courtroom. But it's been years. Anyone who tries to so much as hint at misconduct can trip on a sewer grate for all I care."

Sebastian snorted, but his tone had a heavy edge when he said, "An inference of...shall we say favoritism? Would not be entirely without merit. My interest in you crossed unprofessional lines almost from the start." Beneath this confession ran the implication that Sebastian should have done something to remedy the problem.

"Fuck that." The vehemence in Trevor's voice surprised him, but he made no effort to moderate himself. "I had no idea you were attracted to me. You're a professional, and you were a damn good boss."

"I did my best."

"You did great," Trevor insisted. "Hell, if I'd suspected you were interested, I probably would've done something stupid. And I think we both know, if I'd said something back then? There's no way we'd be here now."

It was a sobering thought. Unwelcome, but inescapably true. Sebastian *was* a professional, in a field dependent on connections and reputation. He was careful, and kind, and he never would've allowed Trevor to fuck up his own future. Any overtures would have been met with firm rejection, regardless of Sebastian's feelings, and a strategic distance that would have removed temptation without damaging Trevor's nascent career. Trevor couldn't quite imagine what this maneuvering would've looked like, let alone the end result. But Sebastian would have pulled it off masterfully, leaving both their professional images unscathed.

And allowing no path forward that might ultimately have brought them here.

"You're right about that too." The admission rumbled lower than Sebastian's usual baritone.

"Hey." Despite the narrow space available to him, Trevor wriggled onto his other side, remaining on the couch mostly thanks to Sebastian's arm around his waist. He could actually meet Sebastian's gaze now, albeit at startlingly close range. "Stop. You don't get to beat yourself up about secretly wanting things when you never did anything wrong."

Sebastian offered him the most rueful smile Trevor had ever seen. "I'm not sure I can turn it off on your say-so."

"You can try," Trevor pressed with relentless stubbornness.

Sebastian's expression softened. "I can try."

"Good. Glad we've got that settled." It wasn't as though Trevor didn't understand. For all the ways he hated how much time they'd wasted—how many years they'd both spent obliviously pining once their careers diverged—he could also picture the myriad ways things might have gone poorly. Disastrously, even. He understood the image presented by the disparity in their ages, the influence of Sebastian's judgeship and standing in the legal community, the proximity of Trevor's professional trajectory through the county courthouse. All these things made their relationship more complicated to outside eyes.

More complicated between themselves, too, if he wanted to be entirely honest.

But Trevor had never let other people's expectations stop him from chasing the things that really mattered. No fucking way would he shy from potential public scrutiny now. The naysayers hadn't kept him away from college, or law school, or one of the most competitive judicial clerkships in the state. They hadn't slowed him down so far, and they wouldn't stop him from holding on to Sebastian Greer with everything he had.

"I'm glad you invited me to the wedding," Sebastian said, nudging forward to cover Trevor's mouth with his own.

Trevor smiled into the kiss, then grinned even wider when Sebastian retreated just far enough to look at him.

"Me too." His chest warmed with new energy, his heart pounding as he realized all over again that this was really happening.

They weren't on borrowed time anymore.

The End

About the Author

Yolande Kleinn may be a shameless dreamer and a stubborn optimist, but she is also a proud purveyor of romance and erotica. Excitable, fastidious and a little eclectic, she spends every spare moment writing the stories she wants to read. If she can drag other people into the pool along with her, then so much the better.

You can find Yolande via her website:
yolandekleinn.com

Other Titles by Yolande

HEARTS RIGHT HERE

From road trips to isolated cabins, business partners to longtime besties, old crushes to new revelations, former bosses to dad's best friend... Delve into nine contemporary romances where friendship changes course.

Collection includes:
Something Softer—Wishful Thinking
Very Close and All at Once
Just About Perfect—Running Hot
Anticipation—Matters of Heart
Right Here with Me—Put It in Writing

AN INTIMATE CHARADE

Cargo ship captain Galin Odona is in desperate need of a contract. When a lucrative opportunity comes his way, he invites Addison Valdez—smart, stubborn, and the only Human member of his crew—to join the negotiation.

Anatoria Baell's contract is not precisely legal, and she has unconventional methods for choosing where to put her trust. Galin agrees to pose as a distant relation during a gathering at her private estate. The negotiation takes a complicated turn when Addison proclaims that Galin is not only his captain, but his mate. The hot-headed lie puts them in a tough spot, maintaining their charade for the duration.

But Galin is a terrible liar. Even worse, he's been in love with Addison for years. Now, through tight quarters and an illusion of intimacy, he must win the contract without giving himself away. The task seems monumental, but Galin cannot afford to fail.

WITH A RECKLESS HEART

When Reuben drives halfway up a mountain for his daughter's wedding, he's anticipating last-minute errands, unfamiliar faces, and an overwhelmingly emotional day. What he doesn't expect is the gorgeous and brazen young man who keeps getting swept into his orbit.

Dusty seems to be a member of the wedding party, which makes him officially off-limits. The father of the bride has no business flirting with a groomsman, let alone doing any of the other things Reuben finds himself considering. At the very least they should properly introduce themselves, instead of indulging the thrill of being almost total strangers. The fact that Dusty is clearly friends with Reuben's future son-in-law should be all the impetus necessary to behave.

But whoever he is, Dusty is earnest and sweet and impossible to ignore. There will be time for introductions later. For now, what harm can a little flirtation do?

EVERY SECOND YOU'RE ALIVE

Major Franklin Cade has spent years fighting the undead scourge that drove humanity from Earth. Now victory is in sight, but it's come at immeasurable cost. He has sacrificed everything in the line of duty—even his own heart.

For six months Lieutenant Daniel Mendoza has been missing in action. Only stubbornness and a refusal to tarnish Mendoza's memory have kept Franklin alive since losing the man he wouldn't admit he loved.

When a perilous rescue needs volunteers, he returns to the canyon where Mendoza fell. He is not prepared for the hope that ignites as he follows a fading distress signal across infested terrain. In the shadow of a deadly countdown every second is precious, but Franklin refuses to lose Mendoza again.

A PROOF OF POSSIBILITY

Aida de Luca knows better than to defy protocol. As comm specialist, she has no official role in a survey mission on an abandoned planet. Her job is to stay out of trouble, ready in case the science team requires her linguistic expertise.

Venturing alone into a mysterious cave is the most reckless thing she's ever done. But something is calling to her, and it doesn't feel like a threat. Even fear of disappointing Jamila Warwick—Aida's captain and constant source of distraction—can't dissuade her. Though it's impossible to tell what waits beneath the surface, nothing will turn Aida off the path now.

SIMPLE AFTER ALL

Noah Fiore, contracts attorney and dedicated curmudgeon, spends every Christmas with his family on the shore of Lake Superior. It's practically tradition for his sister to invite some lonely acquaintance along for the festivities.

But this year's guest is no pity case. Riley Coto is a friend, whose warmth and charm instantly win over the collective hearts of the Fiore family—all except Noah, who remains as dour and unapproachable as ever.

Riley finds himself inexplicably drawn to

Noah. Something tells him there's more to the man than stubborn work ethic and bad attitude. With Christmas fast approaching, Riley is falling for Noah, and there's nothing simple about that.

OPEN SKIES

After seven years working as partners, Kai and Ilsa are the best professional finders in the business. There's nothing they can't track down, no matter how unfamiliar the star system or hazardous the path. When a new client insists on accompanying the search for his daughter, Ilsa and Kai reluctantly agree. How can they refuse when Eleazar Dantes is desperate enough to pay double their usual fee?

But a high-stakes investigation is no time for distractions. Even more troublesome, when Kai realizes his true feelings for Ilsa, his timing couldn't be worse. Never mind that she doesn't seem to reciprocate: heartbreak is the least of their problems as the trail they're following grows dangerous.

With every step forward, Kai and Ilsa are more certain they won't find Eleazar's missing daughter alive.

TOME FOR THE HOLIDAYS

Between grad school and the barista gig that helps pay his tuition, Cole Moreau's hands are full. He shouldn't have time or energy to maintain a hopeless crush on Isaac Hamlin, a coffee shop regular who happens to own the bookshop next door. But Isaac is sweet and gorgeous—and being friends with him only exacerbates the problem.

When a Christmas Eve blizzard strands Cole on Isaac's doorstep, the challenges pile up just as deep as the snow shutting down the city. A power outage, a mischievous cat, and only one sleeping bag... None of this leaves room for pining over impossible things.

Isaac is off-limits, but tell that to Cole's stubborn heart.

www.ingramcontent.com/pod-product-compliance
Lightning Source LLC
LaVergne TN
LVHW051003080826
845145LV00009B/2424

* 9 7 8 1 9 4 6 3 1 6 4 8 6 *